HOME

This paperback edition published in 2021.

First published in 2019 by Flying Eye Books,
an imprint of Nobrow Ltd. 27 Westgate Street, London, E8 3RL.

Text and Illustrations © Joe Todd-Stanton 2019.
Joe Todd-Stanton has asserted his right under the Copyright, Designs, and
Patents Act, 1988, to be identified as the Author and Illustrator of this Work.

1 3 5 7 9 10 8 6 4 2

Published in the US by Nobrow (US) Inc.
Printed in Latvia on FSC® certified paper.

ISBN: 978-1-912497-47-8
www.flyingeyebooks.com

- JOE TODD-STANTON -

A MOUSE
CALLED
JULIAN

- FLYING EYE BOOKS -

London | New York

Julian had lived on his own for as long as he could remember, and that was the way he liked it.

All the animals above ground tried to eat him.

And all the animals below ground got in his way.

So he made sure to avoid everyone.

He knew how to dodge the rabbits, the moles and the badgers.

He knew where to hide from the farmer and her dog.

He knew which branch to leap across to escape the hungry barn owl...

...and get home safe.

But Julian didn't know that he was being watched.

That night, the fox crept up to Julian's house,
and using all of his skill and cunning...

...smashed right through Julian's front window.

The fox bared his teeth...

...and howled and growled...

Discarded

...but he couldn't quite reach Julian.

The fox was well and truly stuck!

"Pardon me, but would you be so kind
as to help me out?" asked the fox.

"Help you?" yelped Julian, "You just tried to eat me!"

"Of course I didn't. I was simply popping
in to see if you were OK," lied the fox.

"I'm not OK at all! Your big head
is in my house!" said Julian.

"Well, if you help me, I promise you will never
see me or my big head again," pleaded the fox.

Julian didn't want a fox in his house, so he went to help.

He pulled the fox's tail…

…pushed his nose…

...and wiggled his ears...

...but the fox wouldn't budge.

When it got to dinner time, Julian couldn't
bear to watch the fox's sad hungry eyes.

So he shared what he had and they
talked and ate long into the night.

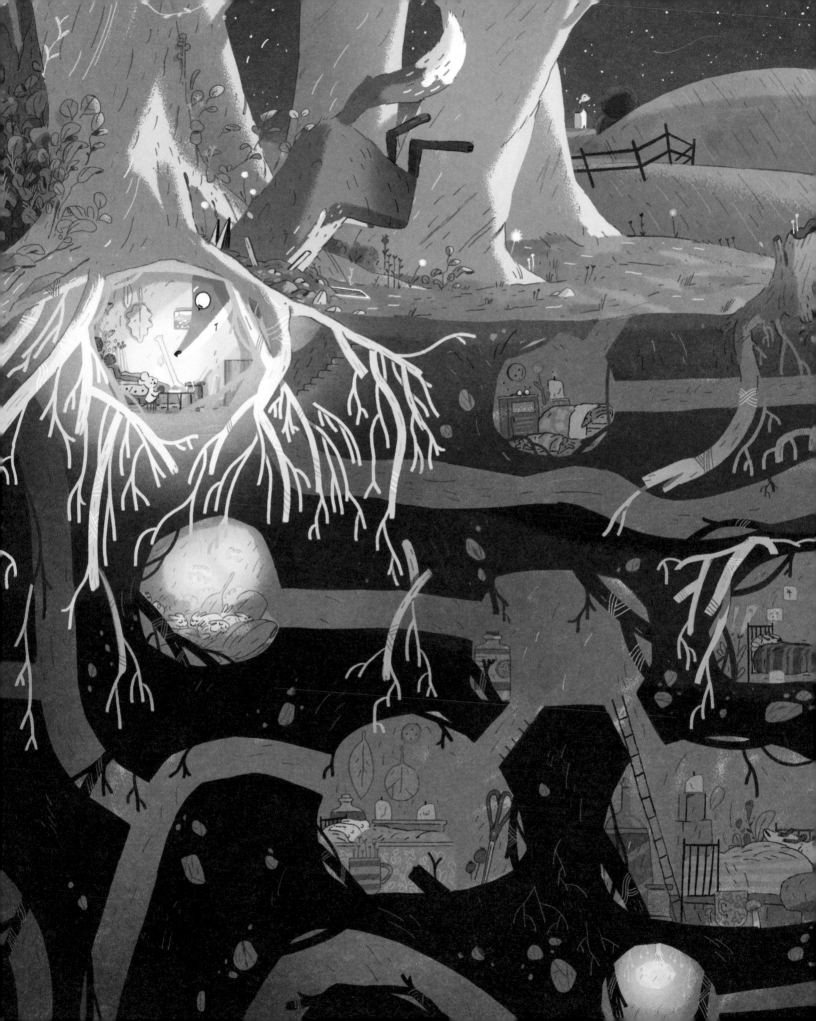

The fox realised it was much nicer to eat dinner *with* Julian than to eat Julian for dinner.

And Julian realised that having a guest wasn't so terrible.

The next day, Julian tried a new plan...

...and with a bit of effort...

...the fox popped free.

"Thank you," said the fox, as he disappeared back into the woods.

Then Julian was back on his own again. Just the way he'd always liked it.

He dodged the rabbits, the moles and the badgers.

He hid from the farmer and her dog.

But he missed the branch to escape the barn owl.

It looked like Julian wasn't going to get home safe this time.

But Julian didn't know that he was being watched.

The fox crept up and using all of his skill and cunning...

...gobbled Julian right up!

The barn owl thought about having a fight...

...but changed its mind.

The fox waited, and then...

...opened his mouth.

"Wow we ware weven," said the fox.
"Pardon?" said a soggy Julian.

The fox put Julian down. "Now we are even," he smiled.
After that, the fox and Julian still liked to keep to themselves...

...but every now and then, Julian had a friend over for dinner.

THE END

HOME

IF YOU ENJOYED THIS BOOK, READ MORE
ADVENTUROUS CHILDREN'S BOOKS FROM
JOE TODD-STANTON

ARTHUR AND THE GOLDEN ROPE

MARCY AND THE RIDDLE OF THE SPHINX

KAI AND THE MONKEY KING

LEO AND THE GORGON'S CURSE

THE SECRET OF BLACK ROCK